HENRY COUNTY LIBRARY SYSTEM

ER FOXE
Foxe, Steve
Meet the singer

Dear Parents:

Congratulations! Your child is taking the first steps on an exciting journey. The destination? Independent reading!

STEP INTO READING® will help your child get there. The program offers five steps to reading success. Each step includes fun stories and colorful art or photographs. In addition to original fiction and books with favorite characters, there are Step into Reading Non-Fiction Readers, Phonics Readers and Boxed Sets, Sticker Readers, and Comic Readers—a complete literacy program with something to interest every child.

Learning to Read, Step by Step!

Ready to Read   Preschool–Kindergarten
• big type and easy words • rhyme and rhythm • picture clues
For children who know the alphabet and are eager to begin reading.

Reading with Help   Preschool–Grade 1
• basic vocabulary • short sentences • simple stories
For children who recognize familiar words and sound out new words with help.

Reading on Your Own   Grades 1–3
• engaging characters • easy-to-follow plots • popular topics
For children who are ready to read on their own.

Reading Paragraphs   Grades 2–3
• challenging vocabulary • short paragraphs • exciting stories
For newly independent readers who read simple sentences with confidence.

Ready for Chapters   Grades 2–4
• chapters • longer paragraphs • full-color art
For children who want to take the plunge into chapter books but still like colorful pictures.

STEP INTO READING® is designed to give every child a successful reading experience. The grade levels are only guides; children will progress through the steps at their own speed, developing confidence in their reading.

Remember, a lifetime love of reading starts with a single step!

LEGO, the LEGO logo, the Brick and Knob configurations and the Minifigure are trademarks and/or copyrights of the LEGO Group.
©2023 The LEGO Group. All rights reserved.

 Manufactured under license granted to AMEET Sp. z o.o. by the LEGO Group.

AMEET Sp. z o.o.
Nowe Sady 6, 94–102 Łódź—Poland
ameet@ameet.eu
www.ameet.eu

www.LEGO.com

Published in the United States by Random House Children's Books, a division of Penguin Random House LLC, 1745 Broadway, New York, NY 10019, and in Canada by Penguin Random House Canada Limited, Toronto.

Step into Reading, Random House, and the Random House colophon are registered trademarks of Penguin Random House LLC.

Visit us on the Web!
StepIntoReading.com
rhcbooks.com

Educators and librarians, for a variety of teaching tools, visit us at RHTeachersLibrarians.com

ISBN 978-0-593-57128-6 (trade)
ISBN 978-0-593-57129-3 (lib. bdg.)
ISBN 978-0-593-57130-9 (ebook)

Printed in the United States of America
10 9 8 7 6 5 4 3 2 1

Random House Children's Books supports the First Amendment and celebrates the right to read.

STEP INTO READING

Meet the Singer!

by Steve Foxe
based on the story by Erica S. Perl
illustrated by AMEET Studio

Random House 🏠 New York

Best friends Madison Yea and Billy McCloud work for the local newspaper.

Madison Yea
reporter

Billy McCloud
photographer

They got an interview with singing sensation Poppy Starr!

They even got to watch her concert from backstage.
Click! Click!

Billy took picture after picture while Madison scribbled notes, not missing a thing.

After the show,
Madison and Billy followed
Poppy back to her studio.
"Does your limousine
have a swimming pool?"
asked Billy.

Poppy laughed.

"No, but it has a freezer full of ice cream!"

Billy thought that was even cooler.

At the studio, Poppy introduced the kids to her team. "I couldn't make music without my producer, Rolf, and vocal coach, Jordan," she said. "My team is like family to me."

Just as Poppy started singing, her manager, the Colonel, burst through the door.

"We've got a big problem, Poppy!" he shouted. "A pipe burst at the aquarium. We can't film your music video there tomorrow!"

"Oh, no!" said Madison.
"Are the fish OK?"
"The fish are fine,"
the Colonel replied.
"But we'll have to cancel
Poppy's video session."

Madison had an idea.

"We could get permission to film the video in our school's gym," she suggested. "Our principal is Poppy's biggest fan."

"That's an amazing idea!" Poppy said.

Her manager wasn't so sure. He was worried the schoolkids would get in the way.

"*These* kids aren't in the way," Poppy pointed out. "They're trying to save the day!"

The next day, Poppy arrived at Madison and Billy's school, along with her team.

"Meet my director, J.J., and my choreographer, Siena," Poppy said. "Siena plans all my dance moves."

"Can you dance?"

Siena asked the kids.

Billy spun around to show off his wildest moves.

"Whoops!" he said as he fell.

Madison helped him up.

"We *like* to dance. Does that count?" he said.

"Totally," said Siena, smiling.

It was time to film the video.

"Quiet on the set!" called J.J.

Everyone got into position.

"Action!" J.J. shouted.

Then Poppy began to sing.

"Cut!" J.J. called.

He realized something was off.

Billy was singing

along with Poppy!

J.J. told Billy to quiet down,
but Poppy had a different idea.
She gathered the dancers together.

"When I get to this part," she said, "can you all join in and sing?"

She showed them the song.

"And can you dance a little . . . *wilder*?"

"Action!"

Poppy began singing.

"I've got a secret.
I don't know what to do.
It always happens when
I'm with you.
I go—"

"BANANAS!" yelled the dancers.

"BANANAS!" shouted Madison and Billy.

After a few more takes,
the director had everything he needed.
"I can't thank you kids enough,"
said Poppy Starr.

"You gave my music what it was missing."

"Thank YOU!" said Madison.

"Yeah," added Billy. "Getting to be in your video was totally . . . bananas!"

Just then, Poppy's assistant brought out some gift bags. "Tickets for tonight's concert!" squealed Madison. "Poppy, you're the best."

"Look what else!" Billy said excitedly, reaching into his gift bag. "Actual bananas!"

The next day, Madison and
Billy published
their new favorite article
with this headline:
"Poppy's New Video Breaks
World Record for Most Views!"